HUNGRY TO PLAY

# HUNGRY TO PLAY

Arti Sonthalia

Illustrated by
Samidha Gunjal

**SCHOLASTIC**
New York Toronto London Auckland
Sydney New Delhi Hong Kong

Published by Scholastic India Pvt. Ltd.
A subsidiary of Scholastic Inc., New York, 10012 (USA).
*Publishers since* 1920, with international operations in Canada, Australia, New Zealand, the United Kingdom, India, and Hong Kong.



For information regarding permission, write to:
Scholastic India Pvt. Ltd.
A-27, Ground Floor, Sigma Centre
Infocity-1, Sector 34, Gurgaon 122001 (India)

First edition: October 2019
This Reprint Edition: january, 2023

ISBN-13: 978-93-5275-985-9

Printed in India at Ram Printograph, Delhi

## A MESSAGE FROM SCHOLASTIC INDIA

When Arti sent us the idea for this book it was a no-brainer for us to publish it.

Kabir is an ace in Tennis, but an F in maths. If you love to play Tennis or any other sport really, this book will speak to you immediately.

I hope you enjoy reading it and it inspires you to go out and play!

Shantanu Duttagupta
Publisher

Dedicated to

*The Lotus Feet of My Guru*

# Contents

# The Report Card

Today, Kabir remembered to hang up his tennis bag on the hook and keep his tennis shoes neatly on the shoe rack as soon as he got home. He was determined to make sure that his mom didn't get angry with him. Not today! Not for anything in the world!

Today, he wanted to impress her.

Kabir already had a reason tucked away in his school bag that would make his mom furious. And it really was a big reason. A doozy of a reason. He had received his report card today. And Mr Madhav, his class teacher, had sent a special note for his parents, but before handing them the note, Kabir wanted to get something else done.

'So, Kabir, how was your day at school? And how was tennis practice?' his dad asked at dinner.

'Good, Dad!' And by good, he meant the tennis practice.

'The inter-school tennis competition is in four weeks and I can't wait to take part in it. Could you please sign the participation form?' Kabir crossed his fingers under the table and hoped his parents had forgotten about the report card.

'That's wonderful, Kabir,' said his mom. 'I know you are excited to take part in the tennis competition, but I really want to see your report card first. Your sister Mira has just shown me hers and she has got excellent grades.'

Even while making rotis in the kitchen, Mom's ear was at the table. Moms must have special ears. They can hear everything! Kabir wondered how.

‘Please will you sign the tennis form and then see the report card?’ pleaded Kabir.

‘No Kabir, first the report card,’ said Mom.

‘Please Mom, please!’ Kabir knew that if his parents saw the report card first, they would never sign the form. And he just had to take part in this competition!

‘No dear, the form can wait,’ said Mom.

Kabir glared at Mira, his twin sister; of course she had perfectly timed showing her report card! Mira looked back at him helplessly. Kabir and Mira were sure that Mom and Dad would not spare Kabir this time. Mr Madhav, their class teacher, had already made a big fuss about it in class. He had said, ‘I don’t believe it, Mira is your twin! Look at her grades and look at yours!’

Kabir was annoyed with Mr Madhav for comparing him with Mira. So what if they were twins. He was three minutes older than her; he was a boy, she a girl. She was good at maths, science and reading and he wasn't, but he was good at tennis and Mira wasn't. But right now these thoughts weren't important. As a matter of fact, the only important thing in the whole world was getting his parents to sign the tennis tournament form.

Kabir's hands trembled as he opened his school bag, took out the report card and handed it to his mother. A frown creased her face as she read aloud:

Maths – F

Sciences – C

Reading – C

English – C

Physical education – A

Kabir knew from the wrinkles on her forehead that his mother was not happy. She then read aloud the note from his teacher:

REPORT CARD

Mr and Mrs Kapoor,

Your son Kabir has not been performing well in class.

I have tried everything possible to help him. Please assist him so that he can clear the next few tests and pull up his grades.

Mr Madhav
(Class teacher)

Kabir's shoulders tensed.

All four of them stared at each other.

'I need to talk to your dad about how we are going to handle this,' said Mom.

Kabir was aware that even though his parents never shouted at him for his poor grades, they still had ways to make it clear that he had to work hard. He started to get goosebumps everywhere you could get goosebumps.

'Why don't we get a tutor for him?' Dad suggested to Mom.

'Tutor?' said Kabir, shocked.

'I think that is a great idea,' said Mom.

'Could I be Kabir's tutor?' Mira interrupted. 'I can help him.'

'I can help myself!' Kabir shot back. The truth was that Mira had been helping him, but he didn't want any more help from his *younger* sister.

'But I can,' Mira insisted.

'I don't want help from anybody!' yelled Kabir.

'Calm down, Kabir. Thanks for offering to help, Mira, but right now, Kabir needs a proper tutor,' said Mom.

'But I don't want to go to a tutor! When will I have time for tennis practice if I have to go to school *and* to a tutor?' cried Kabir.

'We can keep the classes thrice a week so that you can practice tennis as well as work on your maths,' Dad suggested.

'But I need to win this competition! I have to win it because it's the inter-school tennis competition and if I win this, I will be selected for the district-level championships,' argued Kabir.

'I understand this is important but so are academics,' Mom insisted.

'But ... at least, sign the form ... and no tutor ... please Mom, please. Nobody goes to a tutor,' begged Kabir.

'Okay dear, if you say you don't need a tutor, then we'll give this a try. This Friday, there is a maths test on fractions and if you clear it, then we won't get you a tutor; but if you don't clear this test, then we get you a tutor and only then will your dad and I sign the form!' said Mom.

Kabir got the 'Oh no!' feeling. 'But ...' He tried again, looking at his mother pleadingly.

'No more discussion on this, Kabir,' said Mom, sternly.

# The Twin Beep

Next day in school, the only thing that was on Kabir's mind was the maths test on Friday. And the more he thought about it, the more his tummy tied itself up in knots. There was no way he was letting his parents get him a tutor! He didn't want his friends to think he was a dummy, especially his best friend, Dhruv.

'Did your parents get annoyed with you because of your report card?' asked Dhruv.

'No,' said Kabir.

They were not annoyed with him yet, Kabir thought to himself; they just seemed worried about him. They wanted him to do well in school, like his sister, but he bet they were going to get *really* annoyed, and maybe even mad, if he didn't clear the maths test on Friday, and the worst part was that they were thinking of a tutor!

'I have to get my grades up too. I am banned from playing video games for a whole month!' said Dhruv.

'Oh! How sad,' said Kabir. He gave Dhruv a small, blue-coloured rock he had found on his way to school. He had really liked it. It had a grey stripe running all around it. Kabir had never seen something like this before. But Dhruv was a rock collector, and Kabir wanted him to feel better.

'Wow!' Dhruv said, excitedly, 'I don't have this in my collection.'

Just then Mira walked into the classroom and said to Kabir, 'Can I sit next to you?'

Kabir frowned. They had laid out the rules very clearly. Even though they were twins and were in the same class, they would *never* sit together. They had agreed on having different friends too. So what was Mira's problem today?

'Why?' asked Kabir. 'Where's your friend today?'

'She hasn't come to school,' said Mira.

'So?' said Kabir. He felt like telling her to sit with someone else. Kabir didn't mind Mira sitting next to him, but his reputation was at stake. All the boys, especially Neel, would tease him and call him names and say, 'Sissy boy! He is a sister's boy!'

No! He didn't want to hear all that.

'I – I just wanted to help,' said Mira.

'Help with what?' asked Kabir anxiously.

'Friday's test,' Mira announced, excitedly. 'I thought Mom and Dad would sign your tennis tournament form and not get you a—'

'STOP!' said Kabir before Mira could utter the dreaded word 'tutor'!

'No, you can't sit with me!' said Kabir, angrily. He felt like telling her to get lost, but he didn't want to hurt his sister.

'You haven't got your form signed?' asked Neel.

Oh no! thought Kabir.

'Why? Are you scared to play against me? Yeah, you should be! I will beat you again! Just like I did at the last tennis match!' Neel continued with a sneer.

There ... There! This is what he hated about Neel. He was a big meanie! He always found a way of putting himself on the top. Which meant that Kabir was at the bottom.

'Ah! So you are nervous about playing against me; that is why you didn't get your form signed. You're such a loser!' Neel continued at the top of his voice so that everyone could hear. 'Mira, you can sit with me.'

'Thanks, Neel.' Mira flicked her hair and went to sit next to him.

Neel scoffed.

This was why Kabir didn't want Mira to talk to him in school. She just didn't know what to keep secret! She had such a big mouth that a bird could build a nest inside it and she would still go on yap-yapping!

Kabir hoped Mira wouldn't tell Neel about the tutor. He turned to look at her and began to yell at her in his mind, 'Do not tell Neel about the tutor! DO NOT tell Neel about the tutor!'

So many people were always asking him questions about his twin. They were always assuming they had a twin beep or a twin connection.

'Do you have a connection with your twin?'

'Can she understand you?'

'Do you feel pain when she gets hurt?'

NO! There was no such connection between them. But today, Kabir really hoped Mira would get a signal from him and not blurt out anything to Neel!

‘So, this year, the winner of the inter-school tennis competition is Neel,’ announced Neel with great cheer.

Kabir could feel his neck heat up, while his hands balled up into fists.

‘Who said you’re going to win?’ Kabir shouted back. ‘Last year, I lost to you by one point. This year, I am better prepared.’ Kabir was better prepared than last time, but he knew he still had to beat Neel who was better prepared too.

‘Yes, Kabir could win,’ said Dhruv.

Kabir smiled at Dhruv. It felt good to have his best friend back him up.

‘Kabir will win the competition,’ said Mira, ‘only if his form is signed ... and ...’

‘STOP!’ shouted Kabir. He was furious with Mira now. Kabir didn’t know what to do to stop her from embarrassing him.

'Why do you keep saying stop to your sister?' asked Neel, suspiciously.

Just then Mr Madhav walked in. 'Surprise test! Quickly get your pencils out,' he announced.

Dhruv and Kabir stared at each other. 'Another test!' they said, shocked. Was there going to be a test every day?

Mr Madhav had already started handing out the sheets.

In a way Kabir was glad. At least, the test would divert Neel's mind, and he wouldn't get an opportunity to ask Mira questions.

Mira just didn't understand people. She never understood when they were making fun of you, or pulling your leg. All she understood was numbers. Mira was still a baby and it sucked that the baby was his twin and in his class.

'Stop, everyone! Time up!' said Mr Madhav.

Kabir had barely written his name; he was so busy thinking about Mira that his sheet was completely blank!

There, he had failed yet again.

# No Help Please!

'How did your test go?' Mira asked Kabir as soon as they reached home from school.

Kabir was too angry to answer her. He had a burning question of his own. '*Why* do you have to talk so much?' he asked her.

'What do you mean? I didn't say anything,' said Mira.

'Why did you talk about the form in front of Neel? And I am sure if I hadn't stopped you, you would have told him about the tutor too!' Kabir was yelling now.

Mira was puzzled by so many whys. She loved solving puzzles, she had even won an award in grade two for being the quickest puzzle solver, but Kabir could tell all these whys were confusing her.

'What's wrong with that? I was just telling everyone that you were going to get a tutor. I don't understand why that is so bad,' said Mira.

See! She just didn't get it, Kabir thought. She could get fractions in seconds but when it came to feelings, she just didn't understand them—the same way Kabir didn't understand maths. The feelings part of her brain paralysed just the way his did when he saw numbers!

'Everyone will make fun of me, Mira. Why don't you understand? Especially Neel!' said Kabir. The thought of the maths test was already driving him nuts and now having to deal with Mira was making him lose his mind!

'But I was only trying to help,' said Mira.

'But why can't you see, I don't need your help,' shouted Kabir. He didn't like shouting at Mira, but today she would have really made a mess of things if he hadn't stopped her.

'Please help me only when I ask you for help,' said Kabir, sharply.

He saw Mira's lip tremble. He could understand that his words were hurting her but Mira's helpful nature was getting in his way!

Mira said, 'But ...'

'I do NOT need your help!' yelled Kabir. He had never spoken to her like that but he was super mad at Mira right now.

'What's wrong?' Mom walked into the room.

'I –I was only trying to help,' said Mira.

'Kabir, it's okay to take help from someone, if she is good at something,' said Mom.

This was the last thing Kabir wanted to hear.

'Yes, she is good at everything! And I guess I suck at everything!' shouted Kabir and stormed out of the room.

'Kabir ...' Mom called out, but he pretended not to hear.

He opened his maths textbook and tried to understand fractions but the numbers just tumbled and spun, flying away in all directions no matter how hard Kabir tried to catch them. He wondered how Mira was able to catch and solve them!

Since none of the numbers seemed to want to come back, Kabir decided that it would be a good idea to play tennis instead.

The day before the test, Kabir tried harder. He held on to the numbers, he read the questions aloud.

He tried solving the sums and by the end of one hour, he felt he had finally got it.

He tried one last question, which fraction is bigger: 1/4 or 1/8. Kabir thought and thought. It had to be 1/8 because 8 was bigger than 4. Excitedly, he checked the answer.

The answer was 1/4!

He couldn't believe it. Even when he was trying his hardest, he was still wrong!

He thought of asking Mira for help but they hadn't spoken to each other after the fight. It was the first time it had taken them so long to patch up.

Friday morning, Kabir was freaking out inside. He always did before a maths test.

'Best of luck, Kabir,' said his father.

Kabir gave a forced smile.

In school, Mr Madhav handed out the sheets. Kabir wrote his name neatly and looked at the questions. It was a multiple-choice paper. Each question had four answers of which only one was correct. He had to simply circle the right answer. That didn't seem very difficult.

Kabir looked at question number 1. He thought A would be a good choice, so he circled A.

For question 2, the B looked nice, so he circled B.

Then he circled A again for the next question and then B again. His paper was full of As and Bs. Today, the Cs and Ds didn't look very interesting, so he didn't circle any of them.

Kabir wished that the way his paper had only As and Bs, his grades should also be an A or a B. He didn't want any Cs or Ds.

Kabir gave his paper to Mr Madhav and walked out confidently.

# Maths Madness

Kabir crossed his fingers hoping that the results of his test would be good so that he could get his form signed for the tennis competition. If his grades were good that meant: No tutor! More tennis! Less maths! But, and his stomach itched at the thought, if his results weren't good ... he would be doomed.

The results came by email with another note. Mom read it aloud.

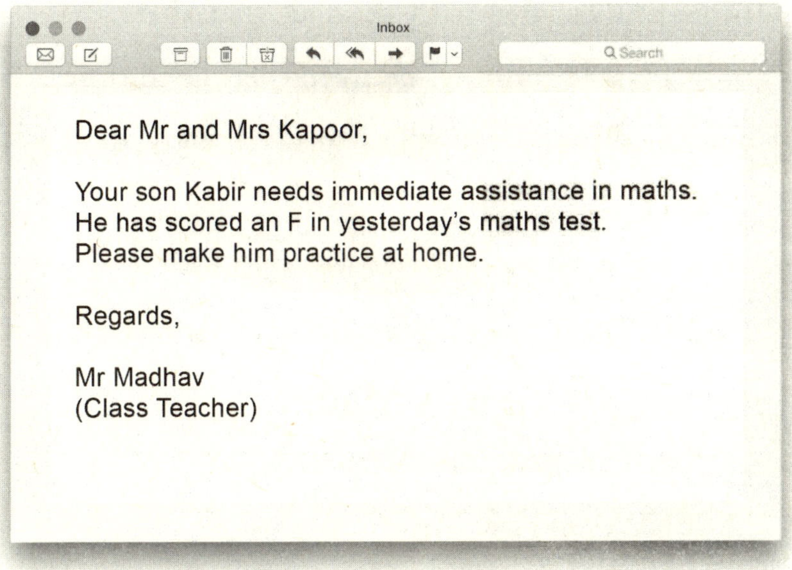

Dear Mr and Mrs Kapoor,

Your son Kabir needs immediate assistance in maths.
He has scored an F in yesterday's maths test.
Please make him practice at home.

Regards,

Mr Madhav
(Class Teacher)

'Mira, what was your result?' Mom asked her.

'I got an A+ and Mr Madhav said I scored the highest marks in class!'

'Good job, Mira,' said Dad.

Kabir couldn't believe it! Not the fact that he had got an F, but that Mira had got an A+. She had to be some kind of a genius to score those kind of grades and he some kind of dummy! Kabir's mind was boggled with the fact that there were only THREE minutes between their birth times, and she was the one who had taken away all the maths brains.

Kabir's hands felt sweaty and his stomach twisted. The tutor thing was going to spring up any moment now.

'Good job, dear,' said Mom.

'Thank you,' said Mira.

Mira deserved the praise. Kabir wondered why God couldn't make brains shareable. He said a quick prayer to God asking him to let future twins share their brains so that they wouldn't suffer like him! But he knew nothing of that sort could ever happen.

'So Kabir, your father and I have decided on a maths tutor for you. She will be here at four this very afternoon,' said Mom.

'But that's the time I go for tennis, Mom!' said Kabir, horrified at the thought that he would have to miss his tennis practice for a tutor!

'Now we are changing that. Instead of tennis, you will be practicing maths with your tutor, thrice a week,' Mom said, sternly.

'But what about my tennis practice? The competition is not very far off and you haven't even signed the form yet! The last date is coming soon!' Kabir could already see himself losing to Neel again!

'Look, Kabir,' said his dad, 'we understand tennis is important to you. But once you improve your maths, you may not need a tutor anymore, and you can continue with your tennis.'

Kabir felt comforted when he heard that it wouldn't be forever.

'And as for the form, we'll sign it only if the marks of your next test are better,' said Mom.

'But that's not fair!' argued Kabir. Tears started to crowd his eyes but he held them back.

'Sorry, Kabir, but academics comes first,' said Dad.

'When will I get time to practice? First, I will get maths homework from Mr Madhav, then I will get maths homework from the tutor. My life will be filled with maths and no tennis! And ... and Neel will win again this year,' said Kabir, feeling a lump in his throat.

'But you have been struggling for a long time in maths,' said Mom.

'Can I suggest something?' asked Mira from the corner.

'No!' Kabir's jaw tightened up. He didn't want any suggestions from Mira.

'I just ...' Mira tried again, but Kabir refused to listen. All he cared about was how he could fit in more tennis and less maths!

Kabir began to think hard. He thought not only with his brain but with his entire body ... he thought like he had never thought before, and the brightest thing he could come up with was morning tennis practice.

'Mom, can you take me to the tennis court in the morning? That way I can get daily practice as well as study with the tutor in the afternoon,' said Kabir. It did mean less sleep, but it also meant more practice and that was all he wanted right now! He would do anything to get enough practice to win this competition.

'Hmm ...' said Mom, thoughtfully, 'that would mean we would have to start our day an hour earlier in the morning. I'll have to drop you for practice and then come back to pick you up from the tennis courts to take you to school.'

'I don't see why Kabir can't go for morning practice as long as he is seeing the tutor in the afternoon. We'll take turns, that way we won't hamper our work,' Dad suggested to Mom.

'Please, Mom, Dad is right. It's only a matter of a few weeks,' begged Kabir, hoping his mom would agree.

Mom was still thinking. 'But will you be able to manage everything? School? Tennis practice? Maths tuition and some rest too?'

Kabir jumped. 'Of course, Mom!'

'Okay, then. We'll take you for morning practice but before we sign the form, I want to see an improvement in your maths.'

'Thank you, thank you, thank you!' said Kabir for the tenth time. But he was worried. His parents had agreed to the morning practice but he knew passing the maths test was going to be the hardest part.

# Tutor, Tutor, Everywhere

A thin woman peered over her glasses as she entered Kabir's house at 4 p.m. sharp. Her straight black hair was tied up in a severe bun, and she was dressed in a dark red and yellow salwar kameez.

She looked like a witch except that she was not wearing a black cape and a black hat.

'Are you Kabir?' the lady asked.

'Yes,' said Kabir softly as he looked at the floor.

'Let's have a look at your maths textbook. Your mother said you need help with mathematics,' she said.

Kabir nodded, wondering if she would really be able to help him. Even if she were Einstein, he bet, she wouldn't be able to help him.

'Okay, let's start with fractions.' The tutor opened the textbook. 'Here is a good page to start. Try questions one to ten and I want you to finish them in twenty minutes, starting now!' she said sternly.

Kabir's mouth fell open. If he could do so many maths questions or any question at all, he wouldn't have needed a tutor!

'But ...' said Kabir.

'No "buts", Kabir. There is no running away from maths. The only way to understand maths is by solving more questions. Now, come on, get started, you have eighteen minutes left,' said the lady.

Kabir looked at the numbers. He looked at them hard and tried to put them together, and just when he thought he had got them, they started to move and shift. He tried to get them to stay still but the more he tried, the more they danced.

'What are you staring at the numbers for?' asked the lady, angrily.

'I ... I don't understand them,' said Kabir.

'I don't think I can teach someone who doesn't even know the basics!' The lady got up and walked straight to Mom.

'Your son doesn't know anything! I am sorry, I can't teach him,' she said.

'But you hardly spent fifteen minutes with him. I am sure if you try, he will learn,' said Mom.

The lady rolled her eyes. 'I am sorry, I cannot do this!' And she walked off.

Mom's mouth fell open.

Kabir wondered what went wrong. But whatever made her leave, Kabir was pleased that such a strict teacher was not going to be his tutor.

Kabir focused on tennis and was glad that his parents were taking him for practice. Even though they insisted that academics must come first, they always encouraged his interest in sports too.

Next day, his new tutor wanted to teach Kabir the guitar and that wasn't what he needed, so Kabir's mom told him to go home. On another day, Kabir sweetly talked his third new tutor into letting him practice tennis rather than study maths! Kabir's mom was very angry with her. 'What am I paying you for?' she said. 'He needs to study maths, and you let him go and play tennis!'

Later, Kabir's mom spoke to his father. 'I don't know what to do! I just can't find a suitable tutor for Kabir.'

Mira interrupted her dad just as he was about to speak, 'I don't understand why you can't let me be his tutor.'

Kabir didn't mind her suggestion this time, as he was sure that they would play games instead of study. But then he thought better of it. He really needed a good tutor if he was going to get his form signed!

'I have spoken to my colleague in office; his son is ready to help,' said Dad.

'Fingers crossed!' said Mom.

Next day, Dad's colleague's son came.

'Are you sure you have come to teach my son?' Mom asked the young boy who seemed to be in school himself.

'Yes, ma'am,' he said.

Mom looked at his hair, which was tied in a ponytail, and the earring that dangled from one ear, and said doubtfully, 'You look very young.' The boy smiled sheepishly.

Mom led him inside.

KAPOORS

'Hi, I am Rahul, you must be Kabir. So you need help with maths?' asked Rahul.

'I guess,' said Kabir.

Kabir thought what he really needed help with was to sink maths in the deepest ocean in the world so it would drown and never ever come back.

'What are your hobbies?' asked Rahul.

'Playing tennis,' said Kabir.

'That's a great sport. Who is your favourite player?' asked Rahul.

'Roger Federer.' Wow! Kabir thought, this tutor was talking about tennis instead of fractions.

'He is my favourite too!' Rahul high-fived Kabir.

'One day I want to play at Wimbledon just like him,' said Kabir. Then he remembered that his tennis form was still not signed, and he felt sad.

'What's wrong?' asked Rahul.

Kabir kind of liked Rahul, so he decided to tell him.

'Mom said, if I don't pass the maths test on Friday, she will not sign my form for the inter-school tennis competition!' Kabir looked at the floor.

'Hey, don't worry, we'll get through it. I'll help you,' said Rahul. 'Okay, now get me a tennis ball.'

Was he going to play tennis? Mom would get very angry and throw him out too! He knew from the last tutor that Mom was not paying him to play tennis or to talk about tennis. Still, Kabir got Rahul a tennis ball.

'Here,' said Kabir.

Rahul placed the tennis ball right at the centre of the table.

'Okay, now can you draw a big tennis ball on this sheet of paper?' asked Rahul.

'Sure,' said Kabir, and did exactly that.

'Now please cut the ball you've drawn into two halves with these scissors,' said Rahul.

Was he crazy? Kabir wondered. Making him cut out a tennis ball in a maths tutorial class!

Kabir snipped the ball he had drawn in half.

Just then Mom came in. 'Are you sure you are teaching him mathematics, young boy?' she asked, sternly.

Kabir felt his heart sink. This was the first tutor he had liked and now Mom was going to throw him out too!

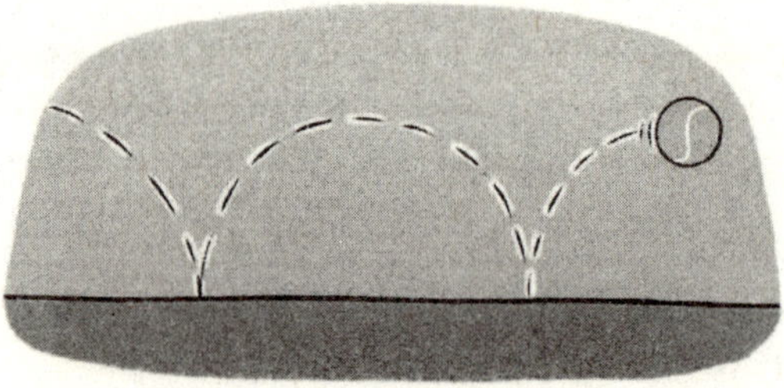

# Oh! Is This Fractions or Tennis?

'Please give me some time, Mrs Kapoor,' said Rahul. He didn't worry himself about Mom's approval.

'Now further cut each piece into half again,' Rahul continued.

Since Kabir enjoyed anything to do with tennis he

didn't mind, so he picked up his scissors and cut the halves into smaller halves.

'Now what do we have here?' asked Rahul.

'One paper tennis ball cut in four equal parts,' said Kabir.

'Great!' said Rahul, excitedly.

What was so great in that and how was that related to fractions? Kabir wondered.

Mom harrumphed from behind them, but Rahul pretended not to hear her.

'What's this?' Rahul picked up the first two big halves of the cut ball.

'Half a tennis ball,' said Kabir.

'And this?' asked Rahul.

'Three-fourth of a tennis ball,' said Kabir.

'And this?' Rahul held up one part.

'One-fourth of a tennis ball,' said Kabir.

'Now which one is bigger: 1/2 a tennis ball or 1/4 of a tennis ball?' To Kabir's mind, the number four was bigger than the number two any day of the week, but he could clearly see that 1/2 of the ball *was bigger* than 1/4 of it.

'Half,' said Kabir.

'Wonderful!' said Rahul and gave Kabir another high-five.

'Hey,' cried Kabir, finally realising what had happened. 'I just did fractions! Mom, I just solved a fraction. Yeah!'

Mom finally smiled at Rahul.

They were doing fractions with the paper tennis ball—all this while Kabir had thought Rahul was making him cut out tennis balls for fun! Kabir had never felt so relieved.

The next time Rahul came over, Kabir learned that 1/8 was not bigger than 1/4, rather it was much smaller.

Kabir finally felt that he understood fractions just a bit better. Maybe, just maybe, he would score better on this test and his parents would sign the form!

On Friday, Mr Madhav gave out the test sheets. This time, Kabir was nervous and excited all at once. The results of this test would decide whether his parents would sign the tennis competition form or not!

He looked at the paper and the numbers seemed much clearer than they usually did—only a few ran away but the other numbers were very much there. He tried to use everything that Rahul had taught him.

'How'd you do in your test?' Dhruv asked Kabir.

'Okay, I think,' said Kabir.

'I think I am failing again,' said Dhruv. 'I just don't get fractions.'

'They aren't as difficult as they seem to be,' said Kabir.

Dhruv stared at his best friend, who just last week had hated fractions even more than him. And now he was saying that fractions weren't so difficult after all!

'What are you doing this Saturday?' asked Dhruv.

'Nothing much,' said Kabir.

'Do you want to come over? Since I have been banned from playing video games until I get my maths grade up, I have been playing board games. You can play with me if you want,' offered Dhruv.

Just then, Kabir remembered that was the day Rahul would be coming to teach him! And he didn't want Dhruv or anybody else to know that he was seeing a tutor.

'Umm ... I think I have some things to do,' said Kabir softly.

'What things?'

'Just things Dad and Mom want me to do at home.' Kabir could tell from the hurt look on Dhruv's face that something was wrong. He bet it was because Dhruv could tell he was hiding something.

'Okay, I guess I'll play with someone else.' Dhruv's face hardened into a scowl. He picked up his bag and went and sat near Neel.

In the evening, Kabir went to play tennis. He did his warm-up exercises and got ready to practice. Neel had also come to play.

'Let's play a game,' Neel said to Kabir.

Kabir didn't want to play with Neel, but he found himself nodding yes anyway.

'Kabir, where is your participation form? Don't forget, tomorrow is the last day to turn it in!' The coach called out.

'Yes, sir ... I'll get it tomorrow.' He hoped he would pass his test so his parents would sign the form.

'You haven't submitted your form yet?' asked Neel.

Kabir avoided answering him, took a deep breath and tried to focus on the game. But the thought of the results were making his knees shiver.

'If I were you, I wouldn't bother turning in the form because you know you are going to lose anyway,' Neel said with a sly grin.

Kabir tried to concentrate but the more he tried, the more balls he missed and the more balls Kabir missed, the more Neel laughed.

'What's wrong with you, Kabir? Focus on the game,' yelled the coach. But Kabir just couldn't focus. He worried about failing his test again and finally ended up losing the match with Neel.

'See, I told you, you would lose to me. It's better that you don't turn in your form. I'll crush you!' Neel laughed.

'Kabir, if you continue to play like you did today, you'll get out in the first round,' said the coach.

Kabir trudged back home thinking about the match he had just lost. He was sure he was getting the practice he needed, because the morning sessions

were helping him a great deal. It was only due to a lack of concentration and Neel's horrid laughs that he had lost today.

Next morning, Kabir's mom read out the test results. 'Kabir, you've scored a C,' said Mom.

'Phew!' Kabir sighed with relief.

'Now will you please sign the form and can I stop seeing the tutor?' asked Kabir.

'Yes, we'll sign the form but the tutor stays, thrice a week,' said Mom.

Kabir knew it was no good arguing with them. There was only one thing to do, and that was to put in extra effort during practice. After yesterday's loss, Kabir would have to push himself harder if he wanted to win against Neel.

# Ouch!

'Thanks for dropping me off for the morning practice, Mom,' said Kabir.

Mom gave Kabir a hug. 'I am so proud of you, Kabir. You are putting in so much effort for your tennis.'

Kabir smiled at his mother's encouraging words. He quickly ran towards the court. He didn't want to miss a single minute of practice now.

'Start with the stretches and a few rounds, Kabir,' said the coach.

'Yes, sir.' Kabir was full of energy.

He stretched his arms, his legs and every muscle of his body. He knew the importance of warm-ups before playing tennis and did all his exercises.

The match he had lost against Neel was fresh in his mind and he pressed himself harder with the drills and the fitness routine. He moved his shoulders with extra force and did twenty extra push-ups.

The coach started with forehand shots. Kabir hit the balls with all his might.

'Excellent, Kabir, your shots are improving,' the coach called out.

But Kabir didn't want them to just be improving. He wanted them to be the best. He wanted his shots to make him win the competition.

Kabir took bigger steps now to get to the balls near the net and ran back to his position to control the entire court. He didn't want to miss a single ball. He pushed himself harder to get to the balls.

'Your backhand needs more practice, Kabir,' said the coach, and gave him more balls to play on his backhand.

The coach slammed a ball towards Kabir's backhand. He jumped and hit the ball back. The coach hit harder and this time Kabir leaped as if he had springs on his legs to hit the ball but missed it and landed hard on the ground. He instantly screamed in pain and sat down holding his ankle.

'Are you all right?' The coach came running towards him.

'My ankle is throbbing,' moaned Kabir.

The coach felt his ankle, then helped him sit on a chair. 'It doesn't seem to be broken but you will have to see a doctor. Let me call your mother.'

Kabir felt something shattering inside him. He buried his face in his hands. He felt like crying. It was all over. The competition, Wimbledon, Roger

Federer, everything! If his ankle had broken, there was no way he could play in this competition.

Just when he had understood fractions, just when he had done well in his test, just when his parents were so happy with him and just when he was getting good practice, he had to hurt himself!

Mom and Dad quickly picked him and took him home. They applied ice on his ankle. It made Kabir feel better but his ankle still felt as if something was hammering inside it.

They took him to a doctor who took an X-ray of his ankle and said, 'It's sprained but not broken.'

'Sprained?' asked Kabir, super worried now.

Dad gave a big sigh of relief.

'Can he go to school?' asked Mom.

'Yes, but apply ice on it every few hours and no pressure on it for a few days,' said the doctor.

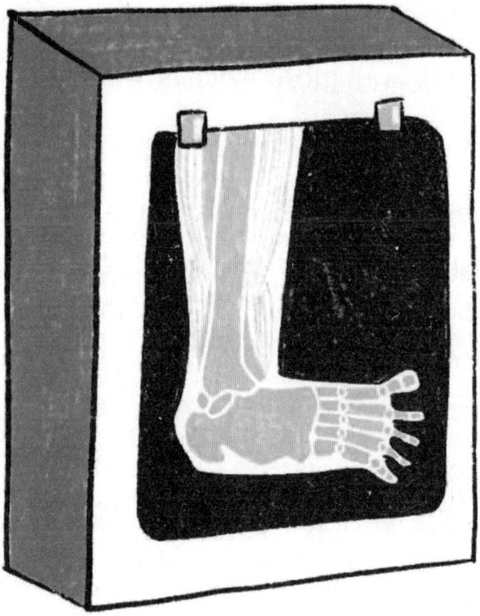

'But ...' Kabir tried to ask about his match but the words just wouldn't come out.

'He has a match next Saturday, will he be able to play?' Kabir was glad Dad asked the question that was looming in his mind.

'Umm ... there is no swelling. If by the end of this week he can walk without pain, I don't see any reason for him not to play,' said the doctor.

Once outside the doctor's office, Kabir felt devastated. He was more worried than ever before! What would happen if his ankle didn't heal by the end of this week? What if he couldn't play at all? He was already imagining Neel walking away with the trophy.

'Cheer up, Kabir,' said Dad.

'I am glad it's just a sprain and not a broken ankle,' said Mom.

A lump was stuck in Kabir's throat and refused to go down! He sat quietly all the way back home.

'What happened?' Mira asked as soon as they reached home. 'Is Kabir going to be okay? Is his leg broken? Will he be able to walk, I mean play tennis?'

'Mira, calm down,' said Mom. 'Kabir's only sprained his ankle. He will be able to walk, run and play as soon as his ankle heals.'

'What about his match? Will he be able to play that?' Mira was worried.

'Maybe.' Mom looked at Kabir.

'What about his practice? How will he manage that?'

Kabir could tell that Mira was concerned.

Mom put her arm around Kabir's shoulder. 'We will do everything we can to put him on the court by the end of this week.' Mom's words gave some comfort to Kabir. He was glad that he had parents who supported his dream. Though right now, his dream surely seemed unreachable with the sprained ankle!

## Moving Ahead

'What's wrong with your foot?' Neel asked the next day in school. 'Why are you limping?'

'I've hurt it,' said Kabir, in a flat voice.

'How will you play next week? Or have you cooked up some story after you lost the match with me the other day,' said Neel, in a mean voice.

Kabir was already upset about his ankle and Neel was making him feel worse. He felt like boxing Neel's ears but he knew his parents would never approve of violence. They would say, 'Even if you do feel angry, you have to learn to control yourself.' Kabir was still working on mastering that art.

'Don't you worry about my foot! I will play! And I will win!' Kabir was not sure of what he was saying but he decided it was better than getting violent.

Neel scoffed.

During break time, Kabir looked for Dhruv. He was sitting near the swings. They still hadn't spoken to each other after Kabir had lied to him.

'Hi,' said Kabir.

'Hi,' said Dhruv, coldly.

'I am sorry about hiding things from you.' Kabir looked at the ground while he spoke.

'But what would you want to hide from your best friend?' asked Dhruv.

'I have started seeing a maths tutor,' said Kabir.

'You are seeing a tutor? But what's there to hide?' asked Dhruv.

'I thought you would think that I am dumb,' said Kabir.

'Oh, Kabir! With the grades I have been getting, I think I am the dumb one! My parents have been telling me to see a tutor for a long time but I have just been ignoring them. It sure seems like a good idea now,' said Dhruv.

'Yes, it is!' Kabir couldn't believe those words were coming out of his own mouth. A few weeks back, he had hated the idea of a tutor but he realised that he really did like the idea of Rahul teaching him.

'Your foot looks like it hurts real bad,' said Dhruv.

'Yes, it does,' said Kabir, sadly.

'Will you be able to play next week?' Dhruv looked concerned.

'If it heals,' said Kabir. The thought that it might not made him feel more depressed.

'Don't worry, I am sure you will be able to play and you will win this year.' Dhruv high-fived Kabir and he felt a little better.

By evening, Kabir's foot was worse with all the limping around in school.

'I think you should skip school for a couple of days,' said Mom.

'But I have a maths test on Friday,' said Kabir.

'If you rest your foot, it should heal by then, and since you are not going to school, it will be a good idea to ask Rahul to come every day this week,' said Mom.

Kabir would have objected to her suggestion on any other occasion but with no tennis practice happening, he would rather do some maths.

Kabir spent the entire week adding fractions, subtracting them, multiplying them, converting mixed fractions and everything possible one could do with fractions.

Mom took extra care of Kabir by constantly icing his foot.

By Friday, Kabir was ready for his test and his foot felt much better. He tried jumping, it didn't hurt. He jogged to check if there was pain but he couldn't feel any!

'You aren't limping anymore!' cried Mira.

Kabir beamed happily.

During the maths test, Kabir was more confident than usual. He finished his test quickly. The results came by email along with a note. Kabir's mom read it aloud.

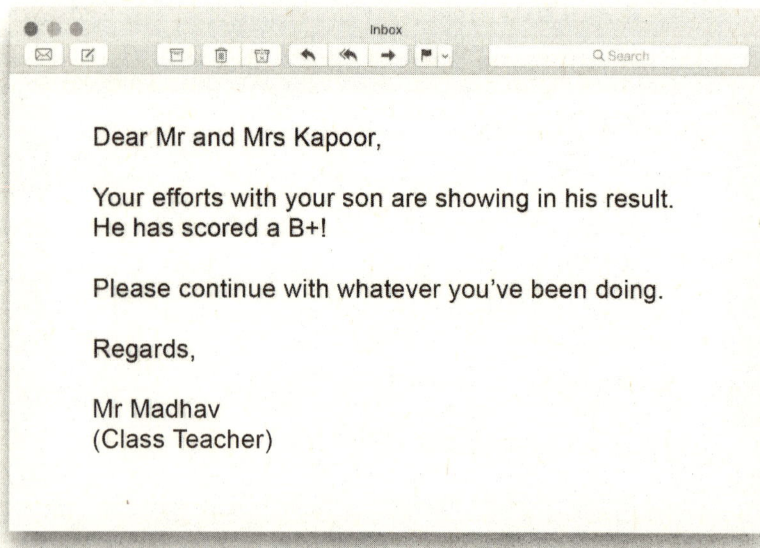

Inbox

Dear Mr and Mrs Kapoor,

Your efforts with your son are showing in his result.
He has scored a B+!

Please continue with whatever you've been doing.

Regards,

Mr Madhav
(Class Teacher)

'Wow! Kabir, this is wonderful,' said Mom excitedly.

'Do I still have to see the tutor?' Kabir asked. 'I understand fractions now.'

'Yes, you do, but only because of Rahul! Why would you stop seeing him when you have just begun to do well? With Rahul's help, you can do even better,' said Mom.

'But ...'

'I think it would be a good idea to see him once a week at least, if not thrice,' Mom suggested.

Kabir didn't like the idea very much but he agreed. He had improved a great deal in maths and it was because of Rahul.

'Now can I start with my tennis practice?' asked Kabir.

'I don't see why not!' she said.

Kabir was excited about playing tennis again but nervous because all the other boys had got a full week of extra practice over him. Kabir couldn't wait to get to practice now. Lying in bed that night, he dreamed of hitting balls across the net, practicing services and pushing himself into every corner of the court.

# Not So Easy

'Welcome back,' the coach greeted Kabir.

'Will I get enough practice? There is very little time left,' Kabir asked the question that had been jumping inside his brain all night.

'Of course, Kabir, but first I want to know, how is your foot?' asked the coach.

'I think it's as good as new,' said Kabir.

'Then let's practice well until the competition begins on Saturday.'

Kabir's tummy did a flip at the thought of the competition starting so soon!

The coach made Kabir do mild exercises and sent him home early in order to not put too much pressure on his foot right away.

Later, Kabir was sitting at the kitchen table with Rahul, his eyebrows furrowed in deep concentration over a maths problem, and then, it was as if a light bulb went off in his head and he wrote down the answer.

'Good work!' Rahul congratulated Kabir.

Kabir smiled. 'You have helped me so much. Without you, I wouldn't be playing tennis right now. It would make me really happy if you would come to watch my tennis match.'

'When is it?' asked Rahul.

'It begins on Saturday and if I clear all my levels, then the finals will be on Sunday,' said Kabir.

'Let me see ... Saturday I have a commitment but I will surely try to make it on Sunday,' said Rahul.

'Thanks,' said Kabir. Rahul had made fractions easy for Kabir. He liked it when Rahul came over, but he would never say that to his mom or else she would get Rahul to come thrice a week again.

Saturday came sooner than Kabir expected.

'Can I come and watch your matches?' asked Mira.

'Of course,' said Kabir.

Mira jumped up in her chair. 'Yippee! I am going to cheer for you.'

Kabir was glad Mira was one supporter whom he would always have on his side. Even with their constant fights and her sticky-beak attitude, Kabir couldn't help but be fond of his baby sister.

The schedule for the matches were out and Kabir was playing his on court number three. He would have to play five matches to win the tournament. If he lost any one of them, he would be out of the competition!

The matches began on time. There were a lot of kids from different schools whom Kabir had never met before.

Kabir cleared the first round of the tournament easily. He still had to clear the second round to reach the quarter-finals, which would be played on Sunday.

Kabir saw that Neel too had cleared the first round on court number two. Kabir was glad he didn't have a match with Neel today, as they were in different groups.

Kabir's second round began. His opponent was much taller and stronger than Kabir. This player seemed to be taking away Kabir's entire strength. With every shot Kabir hit with his racquet, his opponent volleyed harder and the ball returned to Kabir with greater force. The more his opponent pressed, the harder Kabir pushed back which made him tire out faster.

Kabir made a few fouls and hit a few balls out. The score was equal now. Both players had won two sets each. The third set would decide if Kabir would be eliminated from the game and his dreams would die

or if he would be victorious and win a chance to play in the quarter-finals!

Kabir served a ball hard. When his opponent returned the ball, he saw it land out of court. The score was now 40-30. Only one more point, and he would win the game! This is it, I have to do it, Kabir thought to himself.

He bent his knees slightly, threw the ball in the air and slammed it down to the other court. The boy slammed it back, Kabir hit it towards the right corner, then to the left. The boy on the opposite court hit it back. Kabir spun the ball with his racquet towards the net, his opponent ran towards it and missed it by a few steps—Kabir won the match!

He heaved a big sigh of relief and at the very same time, began to worry about the opponents he would face the next day. His opponents in Sunday's matches would be more challenging than the game he had just played. He would have to push himself harder and give everything for his matches tomorrow!

On court number two, Neel's opponent didn't turn up at all. Wow! A walk over in the second round, how lucky for Neel, Kabir thought.

# Do or Die

Kabir twisted and turned in his bed all night. At one point, he dreamed that Neel's ball hit him on the head and he went flying out of the court! In another dream, Neel had won the match and Kabir was the loser again.

'You must eat some breakfast, Kabir,' said Mom in the morning.

'I am not hungry,' said Kabir.

'You need energy to play today,' said Dad.

Kabir tried to eat but he kept pushing the food around on his plate. He was sure he would throw up if he ate anything.

'Kabir's going to win the tournament today! He is the best player!' said Mira, confidently.

Kabir was happy to hear that but he knew today's matches were not going to be easy. After the last match yesterday, Kabir was sure that the matches today would require more than everything he had.

'Best of luck, Kabir,' said Dad.

'Thanks, Dad.'

Kabir's quarter-final began on schedule. Kabir won the match, but he was still nervous. He looked at the scoreboard and saw that Neel had glided into the semis too.

The semi-final match was a real fight for Kabir. The boy Kabir played the semi-finals against was a very strong player. Kabir had to put in all his energy and skill to win. His ankle hurt but he didn't let the pain stand in his way.

Both Kabir and Neel won their semi-finals. That meant Kabir and Neel were going to play the finals against each other, just like last year!

Kabir felt jittery. Last year's loss had made Kabir feel like a weakling. One silly mistake had cost him the match. He couldn't let that happen again this year.

Kabir saw his mom, dad, Mira and Dhruv sitting in the front row, cheering for him. Rahul was there too, with a sign that said 'Kabir for the win!' and that made him feel really good.

Once the players regained their energies, the final match began.

KABIR FOR
THE WIN!

Kabir looked at Neel. Kabir's legs wobbled and his hands shook. He could hear himself breathe. Sweat trickled down his forehead and Kabir could feel all his energy already draining out. There was something about Neel that always made him lose focus!

Neel tossed the ball in the air and slammed it towards Kabir like a lightning bolt. Kabir missed the ball. Kabir missed another ball and then another. Kabir kept missing the balls!

Neel scoffed.

Kabir hit the ball hard this time but it went straight out of the court! The score was 2-0.

'Come on, Kabir,' Mira screamed, 'you can do it!'

The umpire glared at Mira and signalled her to keep quiet.

Every time Kabir looked at the scoreboard, he could feel his stomach churning. He couldn't understand why all his balls went foul. He knew he had to win this game or else it was over! He knew this was his dream. He had practiced, given his best but why was he faltering now? The more he thought about it, the angrier he got and the more balls went out. He could feel his energy ebbing away.

The umpire called for a drinks break.

Immediately, Mira ran to Kabir with a bottle of water. 'This is your final match, you have to win this,' she cried. 'You can't ruin it by getting angry! Don't think it's Neel at the other end, but ME and you know I don't play tennis!' Mira pulled at his T-shirt as she spoke to him.

'Go back to your seat,' the umpire yelled.

Mira ran back.

Kabir had always thought that the twin connection idea was garbage, but today he wondered if there was some truth to it. Because, today, when he didn't understand why he was losing the match,

Mira did. And maybe she was right! It was not Neel who was causing the problem, but his own anger that kept him from focusing.

Calm down! Calm down, he told himself. Don't spoil it, you can do it!

Kabir focused on the ball and tried to forget who his opponent was. Mira's words kept ringing in his ears, 'It's ME! It's ME!'

Kabir's ball landed in the court and it made him feel better when he got a point. His balls started reaching exactly where they were supposed to. His serves turned into aces and he slammed the returns back to Neel. He fired at the balls; he jumped, dived, spun the ball and soon the score was 3-3!

Kabir could feel every muscle of his body heat up. His calf muscles throbbed and his ankle ached but there was no way he was going to give up! He had to move on. He crammed his entire body, mind and soul into the game. All he could see was the tennis ball that flew over the net and how hard he had to hit it.

They played the final set and the score reached 40-40. Deuce!

It was Neel's serve. Neel slammed an ace. Kabir missed and Neel had an advantage. Kabir knew he couldn't miss this shot. He had to get it or it would all be over! Neel crashed the ball again but this time Kabir struck it back and the score was a deuce again.

Kabir served and got an advantage. This could be the last serve, the last point of the match if he got it right, Kabir thought. He had to! He *had* to! He bounced the ball twice before his serve. One point, he thought! Just one point! That's what he needed and he could do it.

'Come on, Kabir!' cried Dhruv.

'Come on!' yelled Rahul.

'You can do it!' cried Mira.

Kabir closed his eyes, shut away all the voices and heard only two words: Do it! He took a deep breath, opened his eyes and released the ball. It soared over the net and landed in the court, but far from Neel. Neel dived for it ... but missed!

Kabir watched and waited.

Chaos! Craziness! Screaming and yelling! It was like fireworks had suddenly started in the tennis stadium.

'Yippee!' yelled Mira.

'Yessss!' Dhruv punched his fist in the air.

'Well done!' shouted Rahul.

'You've done it!' yelled Mom and Dad.

Mira ran into the court again and grabbed Kabir. She wrapped him in her arms so tightly that he felt he would collapse!

Dhruv ran to Kabir and hugged him too. Then he handed him a rare orange and yellow stone. 'It's my lucky stone. I had it with me so that its luck would make you win, and now I want you to keep it!'

Kabir had never seen a stone with such radiant colours. It was even better than the stone he had given Dhruv. 'Wow, I love it! Thanks, Dhruv,' said Kabir, excitedly.

Rahul gave a brotherly whack on Kabir's back. 'You've done it! And one day, I know you are going to Wimbledon!'

Kabir smiled at the thought of Wimbledon.

Kabir then walked over to Neel. 'You played a great game,' said Neel softly.

'So did you.' They shook hands.

Kabir kissed the trophy and felt terrific! He would now be in the state-level championships!

'Thank you, Mom and Dad. If it weren't for you, I would have never won this,' said Kabir, hugging them.

WIMBLEDON TOURNA

And he meant every word he said.

'It's all your effort, son! You did exactly what you went out there to do—WIN!' said Dad, happily.

That night, Kabir clutched his trophy in one hand and the rare stone Dhruv had given him in the other as he slept and dreamed that he was playing at Wimbledon.

**Arti Sonthalia** is a Hyderabad-based children's writer. Her first children's book *Big Bully And M-me* was nominated for the Crystal Kite Asia Award. And her second book *Hungry To Read* has touched many hearts. She also has many stories in the *Chicken Soup for the Soul.* Besides writing, she enjoys reading.

**OTHER BOOKS BY THE SAME AUTHOR**